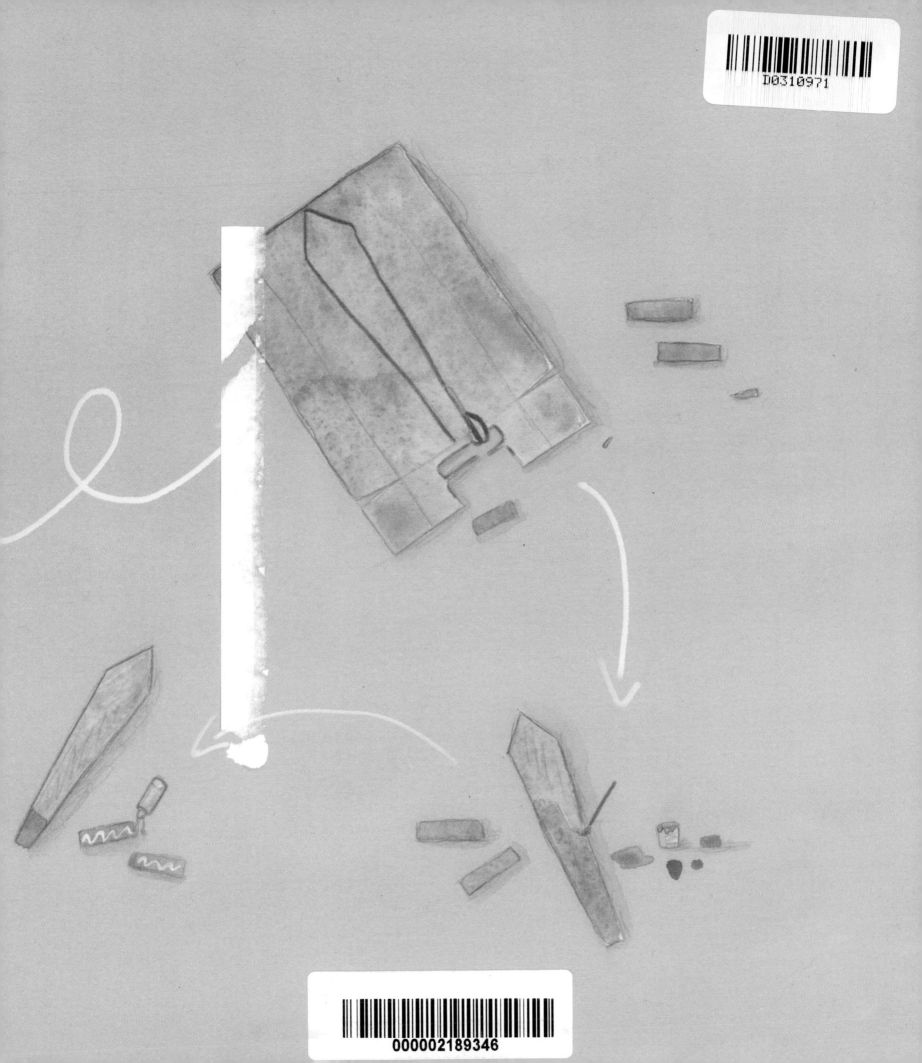

First published in the UK in 2018
by New Frontier Publishing Europe Ltd
93 Harbord Street, London SW6 6PN
www.newfrontierpublishing.co.uk

ISBN: 978-1-912076-94-9

A CIP catalogue record for this book is available from
the British Library.

Printed in China
10 9 8 7 6 5 4 3 2 1

THE Brave KNIGHT

For Josh and all brave knights. SG

To Dashiell and Marshmallow, my little
adventurer and his faithful sidekick. CH

THE Brave KNIGHT

Sally Gould & Celeste Hulme

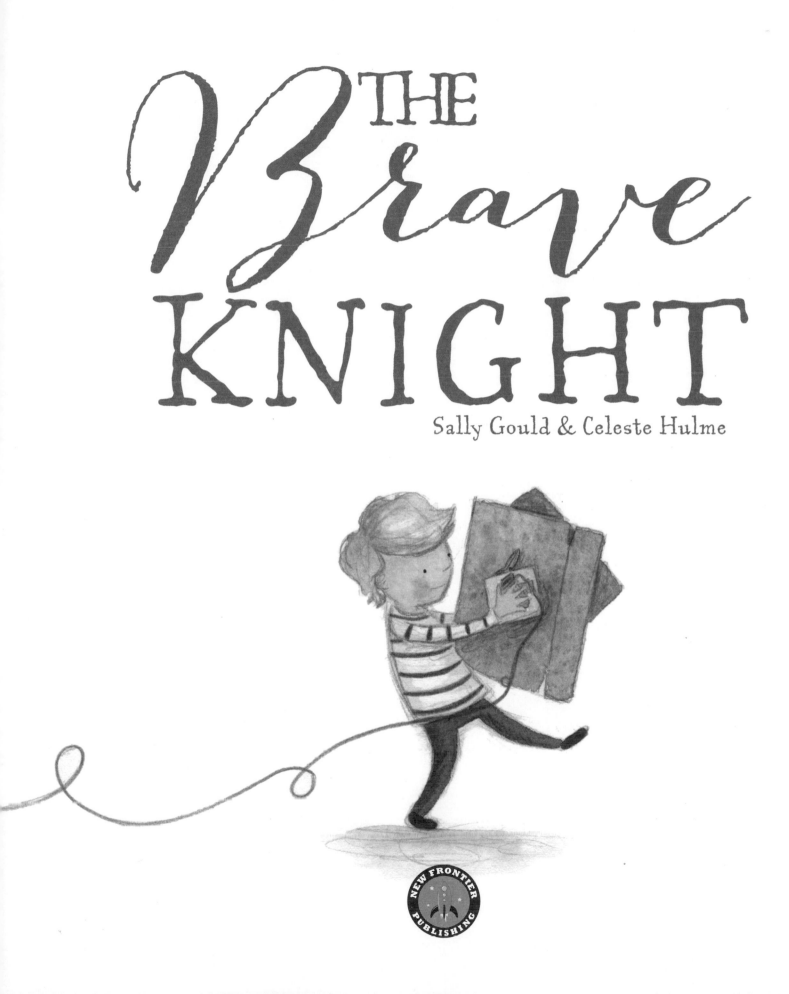

NEW FRONTIER PUBLISHING

I am a knight.
Handsome and BRAVE.

I have a sword.
Long and SHARP.

I wear armour.
Shiny and STRONG.

I guard the castle.
Enemies BEWARE!

I stand still.
Watching and listening.
SHHH...

Do you hear a noise?

The wind?

An animal?

No.
Footsteps?
Many footsteps!
Who DARES to enter
MY CASTLE?

I hide and watch.

ENEMY KNIGHTS!

I am alone.

What will I do?

I will trick them.

I take off my knight's armour.

I look like a peasant.

I go back to the castle wall.

I call out to an enemy knight.

Gold, I say, for a secret way into the castle!

He pays me.
He waves to the other knights
to follow.

I open a hidden trapdoor.
They follow me in.

We go down a ladder.

We go through a tunnel.

I lead them into a dark cell.

I slip out and lock them in.
They are trapped!
I give the key to a knight.
He is in charge of the dungeons.

I return to my post outside.
All is quiet again.

I am a knight.
Brave and smart.
I have a sword.
Long and sharp.
I wear armour.
Shiny and strong.

I guard the castle.
Enemies BEWARE!